# Hop to It, Minty!

*Story by Trevor Todd*

*Illustrations by Meredith Thomas*

**PM Chapter Books**
part of the Rigby PM Collection

U.S. edition © 2001 Rigby
a division of Reed Elsevier Inc.
500 Coventry Lane
Crystal Lake, IL 60014
www.rigby.com

Text © 2001 Nelson Thomson Learning
Illustrations © 2001 Nelson Thomson Learning
Originally published in Australia by Nelson Thomson Learning

06 05 04 03 02 01
10 9 8 7 6 5 4 3 2 1

Hop to It, Minty!
ISBN 0 7635 7794 4

Printed in China by Midas Printing (Asia) Ltd

# Contents

## Chapter 1

# Sounds in the Night

Melanie could hear Copper, their farm dog, barking furiously. What a pain! She'd woken Melanie from a deep sleep. As Melanie walked out onto the back porch to quiet the dog, she stiffened. There were lights on in the back paddock. The sound of a screaming four-wheel-drive engine drifted across the cool night air. Excited shouts could be heard above the noise.

"Dad! Quick!" shouted Melanie. "Someone's in the back paddock!"

Rubbing the sleep from his eyes, John joined his daughter on the porch.

"How dare they!" exploded John.

He called to Copper. "Come on, girl," he said in a grim voice. "Let's go see!"

Enjoying the unexpected opportunity for a trip, the dog ran straight to the old farm truck and sailed through the open window in an effortless leap.

"I'm coming, too," declared Melanie. Before John could protest, she had pulled on her boots and was sitting in the front of the truck next to Copper.

John made no comment. His daughter certainly had a mind of her own. Still, there were just the two of them on the farm, so he included her whenever he could.

As John swung himself up into the cab of the truck, Copper started barking widly.

"Quiet, girl!" ordered Melanie.

She patted the dog and looked at her in admiration. The dog was all muscle. She was fearless with cattle and could run like the wind all day and never complain.

Copper stopped barking. This dog understood everything that was said to her. Copper's eyes gleamed and her ears pointed forward. She was going on a late night drive —and there was trouble to sort out. This could be fun!

## Chapter 2

# Trouble!

As the truck lurched onto the rough ground of the back paddock, they heard loud shouting and car doors banging. John slowed the truck down. His face revealed his concern.

"Maybe I'd better take you back," he suggested.

Melanie frowned. "No way! They'll get away if you do!"

John nodded, put the truck into gear, and drove on. As they reached the back fence, they caught a glimpse of red taillights disappearing down the gravel road.

"We're too late!" John cried, but drove on toward the gate and stopped.

Standing in front of the truck's headlights, they could see that the chain on the gate had been cut.

"Who'd do that, Dad?" Melanie was furious. How dare anyone do such a thing to their property!

"It was someone wanting to cause trouble. Come on, let's go home. We'll fix the chain tomorrow."

Just then the dog ran off into the darkness. "Copper! Heel!" John called after her.

## Chapter 3

# What Copper Found

Copper was not listening to John. She was running back and forth, sniffing the ground, her eyes and ears alert, the fur at the back of her neck standing up on end. Then she started barking. Excited, high-pitched yelps.

"Heel, Copper! Bad dog!" yelled John.

But Copper wasn't going to come or heel. She'd found something. And it had excited her.

John and Melanie climbed back into the truck and headed toward the barking dog.

As the truck's lights picked up the scene in front of him, John groaned. He felt sick to his stomach. "Melanie, stay there and don't look," he ordered, as he got out of the truck. But Melanie was curious. She stayed where she was, but she had to look.

Copper was standing near a large gray-brown kangaroo that lay slumped on the ground. The stillness of the animal told the whole story.

John squatted down and looked at the kangaroo. He sighed. It was definitely dead.

Just minutes ago the kangaroo had been a magnificent living and breathing animal, whose ancestors had roamed this countryside for many thousands of years. It belonged here.

John knew that this part of the country had only been farmed for a hundred years or so. What right had those people to come onto his farm and shoot this animal? How dare they?

Tomorrow he'd go into town and see Clem, the local police officer, and report the incident. But that wouldn't help this kangaroo now. The poor animal was dead and there was nothing John could do about it. He stood up.

"Come on, Copper," he said to the dog. "We'll come out tomorrow morning and bury her. It's the least we can do."

John trudged back to the truck with a heavy heart. He turned to the dog. She hadn't moved. He called her again, and his voice sounded disappointed. "Copper!" he shouted impatiently.

Melanie watched from inside the truck.

The dog started yelping; high-pitched yelps, almost squeals. With a sigh, John marched back to the scene. His patience was almost exhausted.

John stopped. Something was moving in the kangaroo's pouch! In disbelief, he squatted down next to the kangaroo. He put an arm around the excited dog and calmed her down.

## Chapter 4

# Adopting Minty

Melanie couldn't stand it any longer. She climbed down from the truck and ran to her father.

"I don't believe it." John's voice was a dry whisper.

They watched as a joey pushed her head out from her dead mother's pouch. With a trembling hand, John reached in and took hold of the baby kangaroo. Melanie was close to tears. Carefully, John lifted the joey out and cradled her in his arms, like a baby.

Copper also sensed the need to care for the frightened and helpless creature, and stopped barking. She whined and whimpered as if she, too, felt sorry for the joey.

"Can we keep her, Dad? I'll take care of her, I promise!"

John smiled down at his daughter and then at the dog.

"What do you think—should we keep her, Copper?"

The dog barked her agreement. John laughed. "If it's okay with Copper, it's okay with me."

"Thanks, Dad!" Melanie hugged him. They looked at the joey. She was the prettiest thing they had ever seen. Her tiny, pointed face was covered with the softest fur. She was a beautiful gray color with finely shaped darker markings at the top of her head. Long, fluttering eyelashes framed her big eyes.

"She's so pretty!" marveled Melanie. Just then the joey sucked on her finger. Melanie felt her heart miss a beat. She brushed her face against the joey's fur and felt the baby animal's own tiny heart beating.

"We won't let you come to any harm," she whispered. She looked down at Copper. "Will we?"

John held the baby kangaroo up to the light and looked her over.

"She's in mint condition," he said.

"Let's call her Minty. Can we?"

John smiled at his daughter's enthusiasm. They watched as Minty brushed the side of her face with a tiny, dark-colored paw.

"Minty it is, then," laughed John.

*Chapter 5*

# Minty Grows Up

Eighteen months later, John and Melanie sat on the back porch and watched an adult kangaroo hopping around the backyard, playing with Copper, stooping to drink from a water bowl, and rounding up the chickens.

They talked about the night when they first brought Minty home.

Melanie had warmed up some milk for her, fed her with the turkey baster, and made a pouch out of one of John's old work shirts.

At first they'd kept Minty in the laundry room, but after a while, she began to treat their house and yard as her home.

Visitors would marvel at the fully-grown kangaroo when she hopped up to Melanie and placed her front paws around the girl, as if in an embrace. Then they would shake their heads in disbelief at the friendship between Minty and Copper.

Surely, they said, the dog would bite and harass the poor kangaroo.

That would bring gales of laughter from John and Melanie. On the occasions when Copper had become too rough in their play "wrestling matches," Minty would stand on her back legs, raise herself to her full height, and box poor Copper's ears as if to teach her a lesson.

But that rarely happened now. Copper and Minty were friends. Melanie had grown used to the sight of the kangaroo bounding after Copper as the dog raced over the paddocks, turning this way and that at John's every command to bring the cattle in.

The cattle didn't know what to make of Minty. They were used to Copper nipping their heels, so they did as they were directed. But a kangaroo?

"How does Minty get along with the wild kangaroos?" asked a visitor one day. "Surely she'd rather be with her own kind!"

Melanie looked at her father, who rubbed his chin thoughtfully and gazed at Minty lying in a cool patch of sand, brushing the flies away from her face.

"She's free to come and go as she likes," said John. "We've never locked her up or anything like that. She looks at the kangaroos as they graze in the top paddock, but I believe she thinks she's one of us."

Everyone laughed at such an idea.

*Chapter 6*

# Where Is Minty?

It was a late summer's day when it happened. Melanie hadn't seen Minty since early morning. But that wasn't unusual, as Minty would often go off by herself while Melanie was at school and John and Copper worked with the cattle. Then, sure enough, she'd be waiting for them on their return, and would harass poor Copper if the dog didn't play with her for a while.

"Where's Minty?" asked John that evening, as he turned off the engine and climbed down from the truck.

Melanie shook her head. "Haven't seen her all day," she replied.

John looked thoughtful as he scraped Copper's dinner into the bowl on the back porch. As usual, the hungry working dog wolfed down her meal in two seconds and looked expectantly at her master. But John's eyes were scanning the yard, the home paddock, and the top paddock. Where was Minty?

"Tell you what," said John to his daughter. "Let's take a quick drive up to the back paddock before we get our dinner. Just to see if she's up there."

Copper followed them. She would never miss out on a ride in the truck.

They set off, not saying a word, both lost in their own thoughts.

*Chapter 7*

# In the Wild

The sunset that evening was spectacular, with a fiery orange sun and rolling clouds. John and Melanie climbed down from the truck and looked up at the sky.

They walked to the paddock gate and looked down at the chain and padlock. They exchanged a glance but didn't say anything. Both thought back to the time when Minty's mother had been killed.

Would Minty ever be a victim like her mother? She was too trusting of humans, that was for sure.

Melanie cupped her hands to her mouth and called into the darkening evening, "Minty! Minty!"

John and Melanie were about to give up and walk back to the truck when they were stopped by a bark from Copper. They turned. There was Minty on the other side of the fence! They could just see her behind the trees.

"Minty!" Melanie smiled. Her friend had come back.

But something was different. She looked...it was hard to put into words. She looked like a wild animal.

Minty gazed at John and Melanie. They all stood looking at one another. Then Melanie's heart skipped a beat. Another kangaroo appeared from behind a tree. A tall, magnificent animal. A male.

With a final glance, Minty hopped away. The male kangaroo followed. John and Melanie listened as the "thump thump" of the animals' feet grew fainter.

It was dark. Without saying a word, John and Melanie climbed into the truck.

Melanie's voice was sad. "She's gone, isn't she?"

John looked out into the night. He didn't speak for a while. When he did, his voice sounded ready to break. "It's for the best," he said quietly.

John turned the truck around and they headed back to their farmhouse.

Melanie stared out the window. It was hard to believe that she would never see the kangaroo again. But she also knew that Minty really belonged in the wild.